Loolee and the Boyz

The Way Loolee Loves
A Dog's Tale

Written by **Gina Melissa Robles &**
Kirk Hartkemeyer

Loolee and the Boyz
The Way Loolee Loves

ISBN 978-1-7346298-2-8

This book is dedicated to
Our families

There is a dog named Loolee, it's true.
She is a little shy, but that's because she
is new!
Up there in the mountains, she saw her
brothers play.
They played a little rough, so on the porch
is where she'll stay.

"Come Loolee!" Wally said and shook his
fluffy hair.
"I don't think so." Loolee barked and she
stayed right there.
Why would she stay and wait, you may
ask? Oh, but can't you tell?
She is waiting for her mom and dad to
come outside as well.

Loolee's heart started to race so fast when
she heard the door.
"They're here! They're ready!" She gave
alert and barked a little more.
She was so excited that she started to
shake and happily bounce around.
Her mom and dad always knew where the
fun could be found.

"To the mountains!" Her mom had said
and pointed to the trail.
It was the best day! She knew it could be,
and she rapidly wagged her tail.
Loolee's favorite place was the mountain
top where she could see it all.
She loved to climb the hills and trails in
winter, spring, summer, and fall.

She also loved when Wally and Gabe
came bounding towards her too.
But she was scared of their big size
and didn't know what to do!
Quickly she shivered behind her mom,
who gave her a little pet.
"It's ok." She told Wally and Gabe, "She
just doesn't know you yet."

Wally and Gabe peeked around their mom then played just like before.
"Whew." Loolee thought and started to walk, thinking, "Making new friends was a chore."
She wanted to see what her brothers were like, and this walk would show her that. She questioned if they were playful like this all the time. Or were they sneaky like a cat?

Gabe was rather bubbly; he never had a
mean look or stare.
While Wally liked hugs and love, which
showed Loolee that he cares.
Her two brothers always liked to wrestle,
something she won't do.
Loolee was far too little for their rough
play, so that will be just for them two.

But she had to think of something that
would make them get along.
A way for her to play and make their
family strong.
Their mom and dad sure loved her, and
she loved them back.
They cared and hugged her all the time
and even had delicious snacks.

"Come on Loolee!" Her dad called, but
she had far too much to do.
She'd follow them eventually, of course
when she wanted too.
In the trees she felt the wind, and then it
started to snow!
The mountain was truly magical and had
so much beauty to show.

As the snow continued to fall, she started
to look around.
"Mom? Dad?" She started to call, but
they were nowhere to be found!
"Woof, woof!" Her heart started to hurt
and she asked, "Oh, where could they
be?"
She even started to miss Wally and Gabe;
they were all she wanted to see!

"Wally!" She said, "Gabe!" She barked,
maybe they could hear.
Suddenly out of the bushes they jumped
and took away all her fear.
They knew where to find her, and their
parents were just behind.
"There you are." Her mom gave a smile.
Now she had made up her mind.

With a wag of her tail, she suddenly
started to play.
She loved the snow and the brothers did
too! She finally found her way!
They became her new best friends, a dog
pack of just three.
And they always made sure to protect her,
she was happy as could be.

They finally made it to the mountain top
and the view was grand.
"Snack time!" Dad said, and she knew
what he had planned.
Banana bread and pizza, they were
the best.
As the greatest parents, their mom and
dad stood above the rest.

That was when she knew what she had
needed to learn.
That love is something we are born with
and as we grow we also earn.
Her family showed her kindness, always
wanting to make her smile.
All this love and trust made her happy
for quite a while.

Love is like a rainbow; you never know
where it ends.
And because Loolee gave it a chance, she
now has two furry best friends.
As they climbed down the mountain, so
much was going to change.
Her heart was now much bigger, and that
feeling was so strange.

Once they were inside the house, she
quickly found her toys,
And listened to her brothers wrestle and
make a bunch of noise.
Loolee was so happy feeling loved and she
had so much love to give.
That was why their family was great
because love is why she lives!

"Ok everyone." Their mom clapped and they all gathered around.
Everyone found their places and sat down to listen to the sound.
Their mom played the flute so well and so sweet.
Loolee started to feel a yawn and slowly started to rest her feet.

She had quite an adventure, so she needed to quickly sleep.
Suddenly their parents began to talk, and Wally began to leap.
Wally understood their language and his tail began to wag.
That was when Loolee saw their daddy reach into the food bag!

The wonderful adventures of Loolee's life
were nowhere near the end.
This was just the start of her journey and
new friends.
Next time you see a dog like her that
feels rather shy.
Just remember they can learn to trust if
you help them try.

They love to love, that's the best part of
being a dog you see.
There isn't an animal in the world that
can love like our dog pack of just three.
Until next time, remember Loolee's tale.
And know that no matter what may
happen, love will never fail.

The End

CPSIA information can be obtained
at www.ICGtesting.com
Printed in the USA
LVHW050801050423
743447LV00007B/214